Parents and Caregivers,

Stone Arch Readers are designed to provide enjoyable reading experiences, as well as opportunities to develop vocabulary, literacy skills, and comprehension. Here are a few ways to support your beginning reader:

- Talk with your child about the ideas addressed in the story.

- Discuss each illustration, mentioning the characters, where they are, and what they are doing.

- Read with expression, pointing to each word. You may want to read the whole story through and then revisit parts of the story to ensure that the meanings of words or phrases are understood.

- Talk about why the character did what he or she did and what your child would do in that situation.

- Help your child connect with characters and events in the story.

Remember, reading with your child should be fun, not forced. Each moment spent reading with your child is a priceless investment in his or her literacy life.

Gail Saunders-Smith, Ph.D.

D0169792

STONE ARCH READERS

are published by Stone Arch Books, a Capstone Imprint
151 Good Counsel Drive, P.O. Box 669
Mankato, Minnesota 56002
www.capstonepub.com

Library of Congress Cataloging-in-Publication Data is available on the
Library of Congress website.
ISBN: 978-1-4342-2008-0 (library binding)
ISBN: 978-1-4342-2792-8 (paperback)

Summary: Gary the lizard gets to pick out his first bike.

Reading Consultants:
Gail Saunders-Smith, Ph.D.
Melinda Melton Crow, M.Ed.
Laurie K. Holland, Media Specialist

Art Director/Designer: Kay Fraser
Production Specialist: Michelle Biedscheid

illustrated by
Andy Rowland

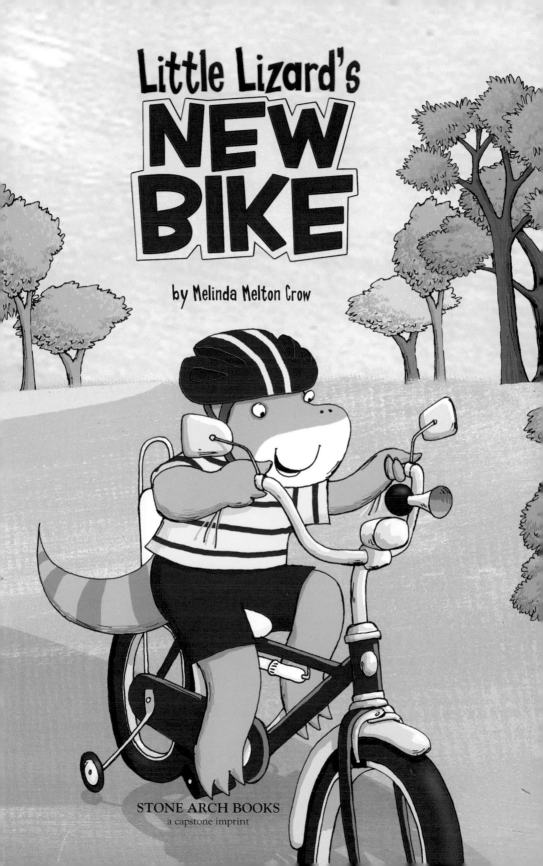

Little Lizard's
NEW
BIKE

by Melinda Melton Crow

STONE ARCH BOOKS
a capstone imprint

This is Dad Lizard
This is Mom Lizard.
This is Gary Lizard.

Mom, Dad, and Gary went
to the store.

"We are going to buy you
a bike," said Mom.

ENTR

9

"Oh boy!" said Gary.

"I have always wanted a bike," said Gary.

CYCLES

EXIT

"I like the yellow bike,"
said Gary.

15

"The yellow bike is too big,"
said Dad.

"I like the blue bike,"
said Gary.

WHEELS

"The blue bike is too small,"
said Dad.

"Do you like this red bike?"
said Mom.

Gary looked at the red bike.

Gary sat on the red bike.

"The red bike is just right,"
said Gary.

There goes Gary!

ENTRY

STORY WORDS

lizard	store	bike
Gary	buy	right

Total Word Count: 103